Wesley Reece:
Fourth Grade Hero

Wesley Reece:
Fourth Grade Hero

Samantha K. Riggi

authorHOUSE®

AuthorHouse™
1663 Liberty Drive
Bloomington, IN 47403
www.authorhouse.com
Phone: 1-800-839-8640

First published by AuthorHouse   07/07/2011

ISBN: 978-1-4634-1640-9 (sc)
ISBN: 978-1-4634-1639-3 (ebk)

Library of Congress Control Number: 2011909146

Printed in the United States of America

Any people depicted in stock imagery provided by Thinkstock are models,
and such images are being used for illustrative purposes only.
Certain stock imagery © Thinkstock.

Contents

Foreword

I would like to thank my family for supporting me, my friends and co-workers for always being willing to read my work and make suggestions, and my students for providing me with inspiration.

Getting Tomatoes

"Wessssley!" my mother's voice echoed through the otherwise quiet grocery store.

I jumped. While she had been picking out just the right tomato, I had snuck over to the best section in the entire store—the free candy bins! I had been digging through them, picking out candy, peanuts and sunflower seeds. I had just stuck my hand into the chocolate covered raisins when I saw my mother coming around the corner; the expression on her face told me I was ready to get it. This time it could be bad, I had not seen the vein in her forehead pop out for a long time. Her lips were tight and she was moving quickly towards me.

"Wesley—I told you to stay next to the cart! That candy is NOT free!" my mother insisted. She swatted away a stray piece of hair from her face and adjusted her purse on her shoulder.

"But Mom . . ." I started.

"Don't *but mom* me! Now I have had it! You have been goofing around all summer with Mark, but school starts

1

tomorrow and your fun is over. In fact, you are not going to Mark's house after dinner, you are going to stay home and practice those multiplication tables. At least you can try to impress Ms. Carlin tomorrow morning," my mother said as she shook her head in frustration.

"But Mom, Mark just got the new PS3 game that we've been dying to play all summer and I really, really, really want to play . . . ." I whined.

I put on my best whiny face and looked at my sister Abby, who was sitting in the cart quietly sucking on her pacifier. Abby is only one, so she doesn't get into trouble at all. I am nine though, and nine year old boys like to have fun and get into mischief. I can't help it; it's in my blood. My mom just doesn't understand.

"Do NOT give me that look Wesley. It's just not going to work this time. Keep up that whining and you'll be grounded until Christmas!"

I decided to keep my mouth shut; there was no winning with this one. I had really been looking forward to going over to Mark's house that night. Mark is my best friend and we're both going to be in Ms. Carlin's class this year. I had to admit, I was terrified. Ms. Carlin is the scariest fourth grade teacher in the entire school. Mark's older brother had her two years ago, and he said that Ms. Carlin made him move his desk away from the rest of the class for two weeks, just because she caught him passing a note. She also made him read it out loud to the entire class! He also said that if you forgot to bring a sharpened pencil, Ms. Carlin would make you write in crayon for a week!

My mother snatched my shirtsleeve and dragged me over to the frozen meat department. I hated food shopping with my mother; she always took SO long picking through packages and sniffing fruit. I especially hated it on my last day of summer break! I should have been riding my bike or climbing trees or anything other than this. As my mother searched for the perfect package of chicken, I let my eyes wander around the store. That's when I saw her, standing in the bread aisle—Ms. Carlin! I ducked behind the cart, using Abby for a shield. Phew—she didn't see me! My mom started pushing the cart and we moved into the aisle next to the bread.

I stood next to Abby, trying to see through the cereal boxes to get another glimpse of Ms. Carlin. My mom had moved down the aisle, and was carefully reading the ingredients on a box of Rice Krispies. Just as I was about to push Abby in that direction I heard a familiar voice.

"Well hello, Ms. Carlin! What a surprise! How has your summer been?"

Oh no! It couldn't be! But it was—my third grade teacher, Mrs. Stall! She hated me the most in the entire class. Not that I could blame her. One time I stole all the chalk right before math class so she couldn't put our usual daily quiz on the chalkboard. She also caught me putting glue on Mariah Jordan's chair one day. Not to mention the time I brought a can of silly string to school and squirted it all over the classroom library. Yep, she hated me!

"Hi Mrs. Stall. My summer was just fine, thank you for asking. And how was yours?" asked Ms. Carlin.

"Oh, you know, busy hustling my kids between activities! April has swimming and gymnastics and Kevin has t-ball and karate. But listen, I am really glad I ran into you. I heard you got some of my *favorite* students," said Mrs. Stall sarcastically.

Oh no, here it comes, I thought. She's going to tell Ms. Carlin all about me and I will be in for it right from the start. I hope she doesn't tell her about the time I overflowed the boy's toilet! Yikes!

"Mmmm," said Ms. Carlin, "is that so?"

"Yes, in particular, I wanted to warn you about Wesley Reece. He is constantly pulling pranks, teasing the girls and he even turned sweet little Mark Ryan into a nuisance."

"Really . . ." hummed Ms. Carlin.

"Oh, and there's also the . . . ." Mrs. Stall started.

"Mrs. Stall, I do appreciate your input; however, I prefer to make my own judgments about my new students. Do have a lovely day and I will see you at school tomorrow," Ms. Carlin stated calmly.

What was this? Ms. Carlin didn't want to hear all the bad things I had done? I couldn't believe it! I heard her shoes clicking down the aisle as Mrs. Stall mumbled something about just trying to be helpful. I grabbed the cart and pushed Abby quickly toward my mom.

"Mom, are we almost done?" I asked breathlessly.

I couldn't wait to get home and call Mark and tell him what I had overheard at the grocery store.

Bread and Butter

That night, my mom made her usual back to school dinner. It had to contain all the major food groups. We had chicken, from the meat group, green beans and corn, from the vegetable group, rice, from the bread group, and strawberries with frozen yogurt for dessert to cover the fruit and dairy groups. My mom thinks that feeding us a completely balanced dinner will improve our brains. I thought pepperoni pizza would have been perfect! What do I know though? I'm just a kid.

After dinner, just like Mom said, I was sent upstairs to start practicing my multiplication. She let me call Mark to tell him I couldn't come over, but I only had a minute, so I didn't tell him about listening to Ms. Carlin and Mrs. Stall talking at the grocery store. I still couldn't believe it! Maybe fourth grade wouldn't be so bad after all. For some reason, I didn't even mind practicing my math that night. I spent a whole hour writing out my facts as neatly as I could with pencil. I thought it would be a good idea to go to school with it tomorrow to show Ms. Carlin. I also used my new pencil sharpener to sharpen all of my pencils. By the time I was done, my hands were killing me! I organized all of my pencils into my new, bright red pencil case. I even put in extra erasers, a blue pen, a red pen, and a highlighter. I stuck the pencil case into my backpack, along with my new markers, glue and scissors. I also added my folders, notebooks and extra writing paper.

Right before bed, my mom brought in a brand new book to read to me. I know, I know, I am a little bit old to be getting a bedtime story, but my mom likes it; well, I kind of like listening to the stories too. My mom always uses funny voices, and sometimes she stops half way through a story, right at the good part, and says, "To be continued . . ." Then I have to wait until the next night to find out what happens. I wish my dad were home more to read to me too, but he always has to go places for work. When I get sad about it, my mom always says that he would much rather be home with us, but that if he didn't go we wouldn't have any bread and butter. I don't know why having bread and butter is such a big deal, but I guess it must be pretty important to keep dad away so much.

"Wesley, did you put all of your school supplies into your backpack?" my mom asked from my doorway.

"Yeah mom, I'm all ready to go. I even sharpened all of my pencils!" I replied.

"Really?" my mom asked with surprise on her face.

"Yep! I'm all set," I said as I snuggled deep into my pillow.

As I started to fall asleep, I actually felt a little bit excited to be going back to school. I especially couldn't wait to wear my new gym shoes! My dad took me shoe shopping at Foot Locker when he was home last Saturday. He let me pick any pair I wanted. After I found the coolest Nikes in the store, my dad took us to get ice cream. I got the usual—bubble gum ice cream mixed with gummy bears and sprinkles. I fell asleep that night thinking about my dad.

Fourth Grade Here I Come

Our school is called Greenland Elementary. It is one big building with two gyms, a big lunchroom and two different playgrounds. On the first floor, there are classrooms for kindergartners, first graders, second graders and third graders. Upstairs is where everybody else goes. Our school goes up to sixth grade. I was starting to get a little nervous again. I had only been upstairs in our school a couple of times to deliver notes from Mrs. Stall. My mom walked me into the building, with Abby on her hip, to sign in at the registration office. She had to bring in my notes from the doctor saying that I had all my shots and some other things that the office always seems to need.

"So, are you ready to be a fourth grader?" my mom asked hopefully.

"I think so," I said nervously.

"Alright sweetie, good luck, and remember I will be right out front waiting for you after school."

My mom lowered Abby down so I could say goodbye and then turned and headed out of the building. As she left I felt my palms starting to sweat. I knew I was in room 204, but I wasn't sure about where that was. I made my way slowly towards the "up" stairs. In our school, there is a set of stairs on each side of the building. You are allowed to go up the stairs to the right of the office and can only go down the stairs to the left of the office.

"Hey, hey Wesley! Wait up!"

I heard Mark's squeaky voice just as I was starting to climb the stairs to my new room. Phew, at least I wouldn't have to walk in alone! He was running towards me, both shoelaces untied and his bag hanging from his elbow.

"Hey Mark, how was that new game last night? Did you beat it yet?" I asked curiously.

"No, my mom wouldn't let me play anyway. She said I had been frying my brain enough this summer and that if I wanted to entertain myself I should read a book," Mark said glumly.

I watched Mark trying to position his backpack and grab the handrail of the stairs at the same time. I almost laughed because Mark is so small and skinny that he looked like he might fall backwards. Lots of the boys at our school tried to pick on Mark in third grade, that's why I decided that he would be my best friend. Nobody ever picked on me!

We walked down the hall looking around at all of the older kids, trying to go by unnoticed. We finally came to room 204. I could see that a few of the goody, goody girls from my third grade class were already inside, sitting in the front of the classroom. Figures, I thought, they are going to try to kiss some major butt right away! Mark and I walked in and picked seats next to each other in the third row, right in the center. I set my backpack down on the floor next to my chair. As I looked around the new classroom, I noticed that it was very different from third grade. Instead of big alphabet letters over the chalkboard, Ms. Carlin had all sorts of posters. The biggest one in the middle was a picture of a big hand squeezing a rock, it said, "Overcoming **resistance** will set you free!" I wasn't really sure what it meant, but I thought that maybe I could find out. The next poster was a picture of a huge lake with a tiny drop of water falling into it. It said, "Drops working together create a lake." I wasn't sure what that meant either, but I really liked the picture.

I started pulling all of my supplies out of my backpack. I carefully placed all of my folders, notebooks, writing paper and other supplies into my desk. I kept my new pencil case out and used one of the fresh black markers to write my name on the top of the case. Last year, this girl Maggie stole my pencil box and put it in her own desk. When I tried to tell Mrs. Stall, she didn't believe me, and Maggie got to keep it. I had to go home and tell my mom, and then my mom said she wasn't surprised that Mrs. Stall didn't believe me because I was always getting into trouble. Anyway, I wasn't about to let that happen again, especially if Maggie is in my class. I decided just to be on the safe side and write my name on my glue and scissors too! I also wrote my name on all of my folders and notebooks. By the time I was done, more kids had started walking into the classroom. Some of them were in my third grade class and some of them I knew from the playground. There was still no sign of Ms. Carlin.

I looked over at Mark and he was busily playing his PSP. "Mark, you're going to get into trouble if Ms. Carlin sees you playing that! Put it away!" I whispered loudly.

"Huh?" Mark asked confused.

"I said, put it away!"

"But I thought that you'd want to play when I got it to the next level."

Just as I was about to tell Mark that he didn't want to make a bad impression on Ms. Carlin right away, she walked into the classroom. She stopped at the front of the room, right in front of the chalkboard and looked right at me. My heart stopped and I thought for sure she was going to make me move to the front row. She opened her mouth and I braced myself to be yelled at, but instead, she smiled at me. I was so shocked that I quickly smiled back.

"Good morning students. As you all probably know, my name is Ms. Carlin and I will be your fourth grade teacher. Please take out a marker, in any color, and be prepared to make your name tag. I will pass out index cards and as your tags are complete I will be coming around to tape them to your desks. Please do this task *quietly* and when your name tag is taped to the desk, you may unpack, if you haven't done so already, and hang your backpack on the back of your chair."

As quietly as she gave us these directions, she began giving a stack of note cards to the first person in each row. I pulled out my favorite color marker, red, and got ready to make my tag. Last year, Mrs. Stall yelled at me when she realized that I had written the word "booger" on my tag. I decided that I didn't want to make Ms. Carlin mad, so in my neatest handwriting, I wrote "Wesley Reece." I even underlined my name as straightly as I could. As I finished, Ms. Carlin was walking up to my desk with her tape and scissors in hand. She looked down at my name tag, and then looked me right in the eyes.

"Well, Wesley, it seems that you have very neat handwriting. It will be nice to read your work this year."

I smiled and said thank you. I was a little embarrassed by her being nice to me, but it also felt good to do a good job.

The rest of the morning went by in a flurry of passing out textbooks, introductions to each other and going over the classroom expectations. When Ms. Carlin said she wanted to talk about the classroom rules and expectations, I wasn't sure what she meant. All Mrs. Stall ever said was "Don't do this or don't do that. Don't talk without raising your hand or don't talk when people are working, blah, blah, blah." Ms. Carlin explained it much differently. She said that she had expectations of us, and that as a group; we should have expectations of each other. She said that her biggest expectation is that we should be respectful to each other, to her and to our classroom. She gave us some examples of what it means to be respectful, like respecting each other's space by not pushing, yelling or hitting. She said respecting our classroom meant keeping it clean and neat. I liked that Ms. Carlin told us what she expects.

At lunch, Mark and I sat next to each other at the table by the window. That's where we always sat last year. We unpacked our lunches and did the usual trade, my yogurt drink for his chocolate pudding. We started to eat in silence. Finally, Mark put down his half eaten peanut butter and jelly, took a big swig of the yogurt and looked at me.

"So, how come you didn't pull any pranks this morning? I was waiting for something extra special, like we talked about this summer. I thought maybe you'd put a fake spider in Ms. Carlin's desk or, I don't know, something!" Mark said.

"I don't know. I don't want to get in trouble and she also smiled at me and told me my handwriting was real nice," I answered.

"Oh," Mark said as he dug back into his lunch.

The whistle blew, and we threw out our garbage and got into line. Ms. Carlin walked next to us down the hallway. She walked quietly and if someone tried to talk, she didn't yell like Mrs. Stall always did. Instead, she would tap whoever was talking on the shoulder and then tap her lips. She led us to the music room, which was where we would be going on Mondays. Our music teacher was standing in the doorway waiting. As we began piling into the room, Ms. Carlin tapped me on the shoulder and motioned for me to move towards her.

"I really liked seeing you work so hard this morning Wesley. Keep up the good work," Ms. Carlin said as she smiled at me again.

"Thanks Ms. Carlin," I mumbled as I looked at my feet.

Music class was ok, I got stuck playing the cymbals, even though I really wanted to play the drums this year. Mrs. Brown said if I behaved and got a good report from Ms. Carlin that she would consider letting me play the drums. After music we went back to our room for quiet reading time and then we got to talk about what we would be doing in science this year. By the time the day was over, I hadn't gotten yelled at once! I followed Ms. Carlin's directions to pack up quietly and to make sure we had our homework assignment written down in our planner. The bell rang and we left the classroom row by row, just like Ms. Carlin told us to do. Mark waited for me in the hallway.

"Wow! Ms. Carlin is really strict and she really likes everything quiet, don't you think?" Mark asked.

"Well, I think she likes us to be quiet, but I think she's also nice," I said as Mark and I walked towards the "down" stairway. "I don't think fourth grade is going to be so bad after all."

Reptiles and Long Division

On the way home, Mom kept asking me all sorts of questions. She was pretty surprised that I did not come out with a note from Ms. Carlin. Last year on the first day, Mrs. Stall wrote a note saying that I misbehaved all day and that my mom should punish me so that I would act better the next day.

When we got home, Mom told me to go straight into the kitchen to start working on my homework. Part of our assignment was to read this really long story in our reading books. Normally, I would have left the book in my backpack and pretended I didn't have reading homework, but since I already had it out, I figured I might as well read it. While I opened my book, Mom brought me a chocolate chip granola bar and some apple juice. I started reading and kept at it until I finished the *entire* story. I finished my last five math problems and then decided to settle in for some good, old-fashioned television!

I flipped around and ended up on the Animal Planet channel. My favorite show was on, Ms. Adventure. It's about a lady who sees all these different types of animals, like snakes and bears. I always watch Reptile 911 too. That show always has some really cool snakebites. The best bites were always from the Rattlesnakes.

"Wesley! Mark is on the phone!" Mom yelled from Abby's bedroom.

"Ok!" I said as I walked into the kitchen to pick up the phone.

"Hey Mark," I said.

"Hey. Did you finish your math problems? I don't understand how to do that last division problem," Mark said nervously.

"Yeah, I got it. It was 15. Did you read the story? I thought it was pretty good."

"Uh—well, I read half of it," Mark said.

"Well, I'm watching Ms. Adventure, so I have to go. I'll see you tomorrow," I said.

"Ok, see you tomorrow."

After watching the show for a little longer, Mom finally called downstairs for me to get ready for bed. I was excited to go to school the next day since I did all my homework, so I didn't even complain about going to bed. Mom read to me again and I fell asleep thinking of reptiles and long division.

Meeting Marissa

That morning at school we talked about the story and answered some questions in our notebooks. Just as we were getting ready to start social studies, there was a knock on our classroom door. The Principal, Mr. Mahoney, walked in. As soon as I saw him I started to sweat and get a dry throat. I thought for sure that he would want to talk to me. Instead, he and Ms. Carlin whispered at the front of the classroom for a few minutes. Then he walked out and shut the door behind him.

"Boys and girls, please take out your social studies books, open to page seven and read through the entire page," Ms. Carlin instructed.

I took my book out and started to open it, but I kept my eyes on Ms. Carlin. She went to the back of the classroom and picked up an extra desk. She moved it into the first row, closest to the windows. She took an extra book, from each subject, and put the books inside the desk. As she did this, I turned towards Mark. He was already looking at me with wide eyes. We both knew what this meant—new student!

19

Before we got caught not doing our reading we both quickly put our eyes on the pages. I knew I should start reading, but I could not stop my imagination from running wild. Who would be the new student?

"Alright, you should be done reading page seven by now. Who can tell me what you learned?" Ms. Carlin asked, her eyes scanning the room.

Of course Maggie, the liar, raised her hand. I looked down and started to read as quickly as I could over page seven. I quietly prayed that Ms. Carlin would not call on me!

"Mark. How about you? What did you learn?"

I looked at Mark and saw the panic come over his face. Just as he started to open his mouth, there was another knock on the classroom door. Ms. Carlin looked in that direction and then quickly walked over to open the door. Mark and I looked at each other with excitement. I saw Ms. Carlin nod her head and I heard her talking, but I still could not see who the new student was. Finally, she stepped aside and in walked two women, one man, a girl about our age and a dog! The classroom suddenly became filled with all sorts of whispers and gasps.

Ms. Carlin gave us a look that meant we needed to be quiet. The class slowly quieted down as the group came further into the classroom.

"Good morning," Ms. Carlin said to the group of people, with a smile.

One of the women stepped forward and shook Ms. Carlin's hand. Then Ms. Carlin crouched down and said hello to the little girl. The girl smiled with her head down and adjusted her thick glasses, but didn't say anything. She just held onto the dog's leash. The dog sat next to her, as calm as I've ever seen a dog. Even with all the whispers going on in the classroom, the dog never tried to move away from the little girl. Her hands were clutched tightly on her leash and she kept her head facing down.

"Boys and girls, this is our new student, Marissa Perkins. This is Marissa's mom and dad and her dog, Jaz. I would also like to introduce you to Mrs. Janik; she is a Seeing Eye Dog trainer. Mrs. Janik is going to tell you a little about Jaz and why she is here with Marissa. Please give her your full attention and respect."

"Good morning class. Like Ms. Carlin said, my name is Mrs. Janik and I work with Seeing Eye Dogs. Does anyone know what a Seeing Eye Dog is for?"

I raised my hand, but so did about every other student in my class. Mrs. Janik called on Maggie.

"That's a dog that lives with people who can't see," Maggie said.

"Pretty close, sometimes they are for people who are completely blind, but some Seeing Eye Dogs live with people who are visually impaired. That means that they have some vision, but their vision is not strong enough to travel around independently. Seeing Eye Dogs can help blind or visually impaired people get to and from work or school. The dog makes sure that its owner is safe from traffic and other dangers," Mrs. Janik explained.

"Marissa is visually impaired. That means that she can see, just not as well as most of you. It wouldn't be safe for her to walk to school and back alone. Jaz is here to help guide her around the building and back home at the end of the day; Jaz is her special helper. Does anyone have any questions so far?"

I raised my hand again. This time she called on me.

"How does Jaz know where to go to help Marissa get home?"

"Good question. What is your name?" Mrs. Janik asked.

"Wesley."

"Ok Wesley, that is a very good question. Jaz has gone through a very long training program and has worked with a special trainer who has shown her how to get around different neighborhoods and what to do when Marissa reaches an intersection or a traffic light. Marissa spent about a month living at Jaz's school with her in order to develop their special bond. Then, Jaz moved in with Marissa and her family to continue training. Now, Jaz knows how to get to Marissa's house from this school. Jaz has also been trained to help guide Marissa around this school."

"So, does Jaz know that a green light means the cars can go?" I asked confused.

Mrs. Janik smiled, "Not exactly, Seeing Eye Dogs don't just use their eyes; in fact, dogs see colors differently than people. So Seeing Eye Dogs actually use much more than that to help guide their owners. Can anyone think of what else would be important?"

"Their hearing!" a couple of voices shouted in unison from the back of the classroom.

"Good! They do use their hearing; they listen for traffic sounds at stop lights. They can not do it alone though. Their owner has to use their hearing as well. You see, the owner and the dog have to work together in order to travel safely."

"There is also something else that you all need to know and understand about Jaz. Jaz is here to work and when Jaz is working, just like when you are working, she can not be disturbed or distracted. Also, Jaz can not be given any types of treats from any of you. Giving Jaz treats could cause her to become confused about her commands, which could lead to danger for Marissa and Jaz. This is a very important rule and I hope all of you will understand and respect that rule," Mrs. Janik said sternly.

"Boys and girls, do you all understand what Mrs. Janik is telling you?"

"Yes," we all said together.

"Good. Now, Marissa, please take your seat over by the windows," Ms. Carlin said as she made her way back to her desk.

We all watched as Mrs. Janik walked over to the new desk with Marissa and Jaz. Jaz waited while Marissa found the chair and sat down. She set her backpack down on her right and Jaz sat down on her left side. Marissa's mom and dad said goodbye, handed Marissa her lunch and left with Mrs. Janik. As soon as they walked out, Ms. Carlin asked Joelle, who was sitting next to Marissa, to take out Marissa's social studies book for her and get her on the right page. After the book was opened, Marissa took something out of her backpack. It looked like a large mirror. I watched as she put it on top of the words in her book. Then she pushed a little button on the top and it lit up. Ms. Carlin started to call on people to read aloud, so I finally looked away from Marissa and back into my book.

Curiosity

Finally it was time for lunch and boy was I hungry! I really hoped mom had packed me something good today. We lined up and walked to the lunchroom with Ms. Carlin leading the way. I was at the end of the boy's line and Marissa was at the end of the girl's line. Jaz walked along on her left side, stopping every time the girl in front of Marissa stopped. When we got to the lunchroom, Ms. Carlin led us to our two regular tables. We are allowed to sit with our friends at lunch, as long as we don't get too loud or get into trouble. Last year, I spent the last few weeks of school sitting at a desk against the far wall because I started a minor food fight that ended with one of the lunchroom monitors getting a soda shower. I was not about to let that happen again!

I saw Mark sitting by the window. He had saved my seat. I sat down next to him and opened my lunch to see what my mom had packed. I pulled out my sandwich and saw that it was ham and mustard. She also packed apple slices, my yogurt drink and a box of apple juice. I traded Mark my yogurt for his pudding and dug right into the sandwich. After eating for a few minutes, I looked down at the end of our table and noticed Marissa and Jaz. Marissa was eating a sandwich and Jaz was sitting at her feet. None of the other girls in our class were sitting with her. In fact, most of them were crowded around the other table. I felt bad that she was sitting alone, but boys and girls didn't usually talk to each other during lunch, or any other time for that matter.

For the rest of lunch Mark and I talked about video games and made plans to get together and play them over the weekend. I hoped my mom would let me go over there since I was behaving so well in school! My dad was coming home this weekend though, so I was also hoping that we could all do something fun together. I had been asking to go to the zoo or the aquarium, so maybe I could convince my mom and dad to do that.

We went outside for recess and did the usual activities. Mark and I played basketball with two of the boys from the other fourth grade class. All the girls either played on the swings and monkey bars or sat around in little groups whispering to each other. I did not understand why girls always had to tell secrets. They acted so strange and were always getting into arguments with their best friends and crying and then making up later that day. I definitely did not understand girls at all. After we played for a while, I noticed Marissa and Jaz walking around in the grass. She was alone again and she looked a little sad this time.

The afternoon went by quickly. We went to gym and played kickball and then read from our science books. Before

I knew it, Ms. Carlin was having us pack up and write down our homework. We had math and we had to write about a current event. I always loved those assignments because it meant I had to watch TV! Mark and I walked down the stairs together and then said goodbye at the back doors where his mom was waiting. My mom had to take Abby to the doctor today, so she told me to walk home. I didn't mind because it was only four or five blocks and I had my IPOD with me. I picked some music and started on my way.

After I got about a block away from school, I noticed Marissa and Jaz walking in front of me. I still couldn't believe that Jaz had learned how to get her home and all around the neighborhood and school. I didn't mean to, but I started following them, not just because I wanted to see her stop at all the street corners and listen for cars, but also because it was the way to my house. I kept on walking behind them, but I didn't say anything. Finally, we were in front of my house. I saw that my mom's car wasn't in the driveway yet, so I stayed behind them and passed by my house. They walked another block and then Jaz turned, with Marissa behind her, into the driveway of their house. I saw Marissa reach into the front pocket on her backpack and pull out keys. She found the right one and she and Jaz disappeared into the house. I stood there for a minute, and then turned around and started walking the block towards home. I took one final glance at her house and thought I saw a shadow looking out the front window, but the sun was glaring in my eyes so I had to turn away. By the time I got home, I was ready for a snack and some TV.

27

Close Call

The next morning, I asked Mom if I could walk to school and she said yes. I was secretly hoping to see Marissa and Jaz again. This time, I wanted to say hi to her. I felt bad that she seemed lonely. I walked down the driveway and looked in the direction of her house, but didn't see anything. I started on my way and noticed someone walking a dog way down the block. I thought it might be them, so I picked up my pace to catch up.

As I got closer I saw that it was Marissa and Jaz. I quickened my pace even more and finally caught up to them. "Hey, Marissa, I'm Wesley from your class," I said.

Marissa stopped walking and looked in my direction. I stopped too. "Oh yeah, hi."

"How's it going? Do you like your new house?" I asked cautiously.

Marissa turned her head towards me, but kept her eyes down. Her thick glasses reflected the sunlight.

"It's really nice, but I'm still getting used to where everything is. Um, were you walking behind us yesterday?"

I felt my face turning red and hot, but I didn't want to lie. "Yeah, sorry—I was just watching how Jaz knows to stop at all the intersections," I explained.

"It's ok," Marissa shrugged as she started to walk again.

"So, is anyone ever allowed to pet Jaz?" I wondered out loud.

"Yeah, but only when she's not guiding me and if I give the "OK" command. Otherwise she can get confused. Do you want to pet her?"

"Sure!" I exclaimed.

Marissa stopped walking again and told Jaz to sit. She said, "Ok Jaz," and then told me I could pet her. I stooped down and looked into her big eyes. I let her sniff my hand first and then I reached out to pet her. Her fur was very soft and she closed her eyes under the touch of my hand. Then she licked my fingers. I laughed and told Marissa.

"She must like you," Marissa said.

"What kind of dog is she?" I asked.

"She's a Golden Retriever and she was born to be a service dog, which means a dog that helps people with disabilities," Marissa said as we started walking again.

The rest of the walk to school Marissa talked all about how her parents signed her up to get a service dog and how long it took. She said when she first came to the training building, Jaz ran straight to her. The trainers knew they had found a good match. Marissa and her mother lived at the school for a month and learned all about how to train Jaz. Marissa has had her now for six months.

We finally got to the last street to cross before we would be in the field next to our school. I watched as Jaz sat down to help Marissa know there was a street. Jaz started to get up to cross just as a car came screeching around the corner! I grabbed Jaz's leash and yelled, "Wait!"

Jaz stopped and pulled back and Marissa jumped a little. The driver blasted the horn and kept on going. I could see a bunch of older kids in the backseat laughing and pointing as they went by.

"Are you ok?" I asked Marissa.

"Yeah, I think so."

She bent down to feel over Jaz, who didn't seem upset by any of it. My heart was racing! My hands felt a little shaky too. We double checked the street, crossed and made our way to school. I looked over at Marissa as we walked in and could see that she was scared. Her lower lip was quivering like she was trying not to cry.

The rest of the school day was pretty uneventful. We started talking about the branches of government in social studies and the food chain in science. I could care less about the government stuff, but I liked learning about predators and prey in the food chain. I looked at Marissa a couple of times throughout the day. She kept looking at Jaz and didn't seem to be paying much attention to Ms. Carlin. When I was packing up at the end of the day, I saw Ms. Carlin pull her aside. Marissa started crying! I wanted to stay and see what was going on, but the bell rang and Ms. Carlin dismissed us.

Mark and I walked downstairs and out the door to find our moms. I spotted my mom and Abby waiting by our car. Marissa and Jaz hadn't come out yet, so I just walked over the car and got in the front seat. Mom put Abby into her car seat, got in herself and we took off.

"So, what did you do in school today?" Mom asked cheerfully.

"Nothing much."

Mom checked her mirrors and switched lanes to turn onto Cedar. We drove for a while, Mom was singing quietly to herself. The song ended and she finally turned down the radio.

"Did you get in trouble with Ms. Carlin or one of the other teachers?" Mom asked with worry in her voice.

"No, why do you think that?" I asked quickly.

"Well, you just seem a little unhappy this afternoon."

"No," I muttered.

"Alright, well, Dad is gone until tomorrow and I really don't feel like cooking. What do you say we stop and pick up a pizza and a movie?"

"Really?" I asked.

"Sure. We can even get pepperoni if you want."

I smiled and was about to tell her about Marissa and Jaz when Abby started making all sorts of gurgling noises. Mom and I laughed. Mom started making up a little song about pepperoni pizza and I forgot about the close call with the car that morning.

Rescue Mission

The next day, Marissa didn't come to school. She didn't come the day after that either. In fact, she was absent for almost a week. I walked by her house a couple of times, but the shades were always closed and I didn't see her parents' car in the driveway either. I was beginning to think she moved away. School went by as usual. Mark got in trouble for playing his PSP in class and Ms. Carlin took it away until Christmas Break. Maggie tried to steal my new box of colored pencils, but Ms. Carlin caught her because I had written my name on the box. Ms. Carlin called Maggie's mom and her mom made her apologize to me and promise she would never go into my desk again. I only half believed her!

After school on Wednesday, I was supposed to walk home because my mom was taking Abby to get her first haircut. I knew they wouldn't be home for a while so Mark and I stayed after school and played basketball outside. We shot around for a little while. Mark missed most of the shots and I made most of mine, but I never gave him a hard time about it.

"Hey Mark, it's almost 4:30, I need to go before my mom gets home with Abby. I was supposed to take out the garbage after school."

"Ok, I have to go too. My mom is already mad about me playing my PSP at school."

"See you tomorrow," I said as I turned towards home dribbling my basketball.

"Yeah, see you."

I walked around the school and through the playground. I thought I heard some kids laughing somewhere, but I couldn't see anyone. I kept walking, but as I got close to the edge of the field I saw Marissa and Jaz in the distance. They were up against the wall of the senior center, which was across the street from our school. Marissa was gripping Jaz's leash and Jaz was standing in front of her, really low to ground. I could see her starting to show her teeth. Marissa had her head hung low. In front of Marissa and Jaz were two older boys. They were calling Marissa names and they were throwing rocks at Jaz! I looked around for help, but there was nobody in sight. I looked back and realized that the car parked in the senior center parking lot was the same car that almost hit us a week ago. The boys kept laughing and tossing rocks and Marissa was starting to cry. It looked like Jaz had blood on her front leg. I didn't know what to do, but I knew that I had to do something. I ran around the other side of the building so they wouldn't see me and looked around for something that could help Marissa and

Jaz. I looked towards the car and saw that the windows were open. I ran over and jumped in through the passenger side. I don't know much about cars, but I do know how the horn works! I pushed down on the steering wheel as hard as I could and blasted the horn! Both of the boys turned and looked towards me. I waved from inside the car and they both started running towards me and the car. As soon as they turned away from Marissa, Jaz started guiding her in the opposite direction. I jumped out of the car and started running away from Marissa and Jaz so the boys would follow me and they would have a chance to escape. It worked! Except now I had to outrun two teenagers! I threw my basketball back in their direction and ran as fast as I could. Luckily, this was my neighborhood and I knew all the yards without fences.

I ran through two backyards and came out on the opposite street. I started running towards home. I looked back and thought that I had lost them so I started to slow down. I made it another half block or so when I heard the sound of screeching tires. I turned around and saw that it was them! I started running again, this time cutting through two more yards to get to my own street. I was only a few houses away from home and the car was gaining on me. Just as I was about to run to my front door, the car pulled up into my driveway and blocked me. The boys got out and they did not look happy!

"Hey! Get outta here right now before I call the police!"

I looked up and saw my dad walking towards us, a serious look on his face! Phew! I was always happy when my dad got home from a business trip, but I had never been this happy!

"Dad!" I yelled as I ran towards him.

I ran to him and he put his big arm protectively over my shoulder. I memorized the license plate as the car peeled out of our driveway. I told my parents the whole story, starting with how they almost ran us down a week ago. My dad called the police and then he called Marissa's parents. Marissa's parents said Marissa and Jaz were fine, but Jaz had to go to the veterinarian to get some stitches in her leg. They said Jaz would be as good as new in a few days. Marissa was pretty scared, but she was going to come back to school as soon as Jaz was better. In the meantime, her parents asked if I could bring her homework by after school. I was happy about that because I really wanted to talk to her and to see Jaz.

Mom and Dad were so proud of me for standing up to the boys and for helping out Marissa and Jaz that they said I could pick out any video game at the store. I thought about it long and hard, but realized that there was only one thing that I really wanted and that was a dog of my own! Mom seemed a little unsure, but Dad thought it was a great idea. They said we could go down to the shelter and pick one out that weekend.

The next day at school, everyone was talking about how I rescued Marissa and Jaz. Ms. Carlin was so happy that she said I could be Marissa's official helper at school. That means I get to leave a few minutes early with her and Jaz to get out before all the students crowd the hallways.

Ms. Carlin also heard what happened to the two teenagers who were harassing Marissa and Jaz. The police went to the house of the boy whose car it was and got him to tell them his friend's name. They arrested both boys and took them to the police station for fingerprinting. Their parents were told and both boys have to go to court for animal cruelty. Ms. Carlin said they would probably have to pay a fine and do community service. Something tells me they won't be bothering Marissa and Jaz again!

After school I walked to Marissa's house with her homework as promised. Her mom let me in. She took me into their family room where Marissa was reading a book with her magnifying light. Jaz was on the floor by her feet. When she saw me, she jumped up and ran over.

"Can I pet her?"

"Sure. Jaz it's ok."

I crouched down and Jaz licked me across the nose. I stroked her back for a few minutes and hugged her around her neck.

"Here's your homework. Everyone at school says hi and they're really glad you and Jaz are ok."

"Thanks," Marissa said quietly.

"Are you ok?"

"Yeah, I was just so scared that those boys were going to hurt Jaz or take her from me. I know she wants to protect me, but I want to protect her too."

"I know. I don't think those boys are going to bother you anymore though. They got into big trouble! And now I can walk with you and Jaz too if you want, we can all look out for each other."

"That would be good. Thanks. Hey, my mom said your parents are letting you get a dog too. What are you going to name it?"

"Well, we're going to the shelter this weekend to pick one out. I guess I'll have to see what it looks like before I can pick a name. Do you want to come with us?"

"Sure. Can Jaz come too?"

"I think so. I want Jaz to like my dog so they can play when Jaz is off duty. I'll ask my mom."

"Marissa! It's time to do homework!" Marissa's mom called from the kitchen.

"Ok! I'll be right there."

"Well, I need to go anyway. My dad is still home and we're going to go out for pizza tonight."

"Thanks for bringing my homework over."

"No problem."

"Oh, and Wesley?"

"Yeah?"

"Thanks for helping us get away the other day. I don't know what I would have done if you hadn't come along."

"Anytime."

Finding Ozzi

That Saturday morning we stopped by Marissa's house to let them know we were leaving for the shelter. Marissa's parents decided to come too, so we had to take two cars. I was so excited about picking out my very own dog that I hadn't been able to sleep at all the night before. Mom said the only rule was that the dog had to be really gentle with Abby.

When we walked in we had to fill out some papers. Marissa and her family had to wait up front so there weren't too many people walking through the kennels. Plus, Jaz had to wait until I picked my dog. Mom, Dad, Abby and I walked in through the doors leading to where all the dogs were kept. There were lots of dogs to choose from, but I knew I would know the right dog when I saw it.

We passed by a cage full of black and white puppies, an older Greyhound, a few Labradors and finally we stopped in front of the cage of a goofy-looking, slobbery brown dog. The sign on the cage said, "My name is Ozzi and I am a two year old Boxer/Rhodesian Ridgeback mix. I am good with other animals and kids. I love a good belly rub and to go for long walks. I need lots of exercise and fun."

"This is him," I said.

"Well, let's take him out and see if he's the right match for our family," Dad said.

One of the volunteers took Ozzi out and brought him to a small room. As soon as Ozzi was let off the leash, he ran around sniffing all of us. He licked Abby across the face and ran over to me. I rubbed his head and played with him for a while and I knew I wanted Ozzi to come home with us. There was just one more test he had to pass: Jaz. My Dad went and told Marissa she could bring her in now. As soon as Jaz entered, Ozzi ran right up to her and started sniffing her. Marissa gave the ok command and released Jaz to meet Ozzi. They walked around in circles for a while, sniffing each other, and then they started to play. They looked like they were wrestling, but in a friendly way. I looked over at Marissa and even though I knew she couldn't see Jaz and Ozzi as clearly as I could, she could tell they were on their way to becoming friends.

About the Author

Samantha K. Riggi currently lives near Chicago with her husband and their two children. She enjoys writing children's books and poetry. She is also an elementary school teacher.

Made in the USA
Lexington, KY
13 December 2011